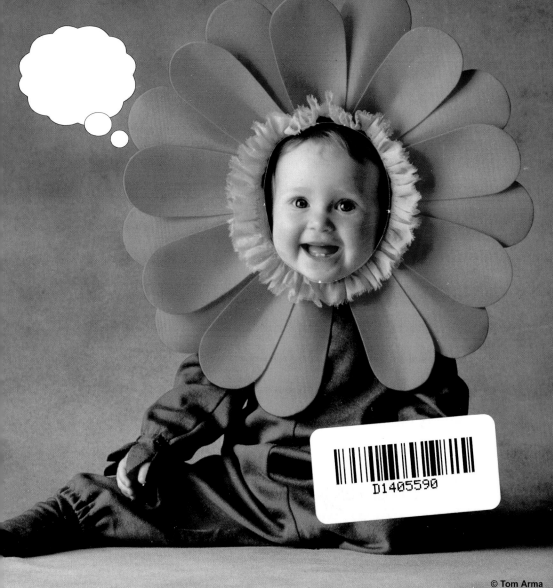

© Tom Arma

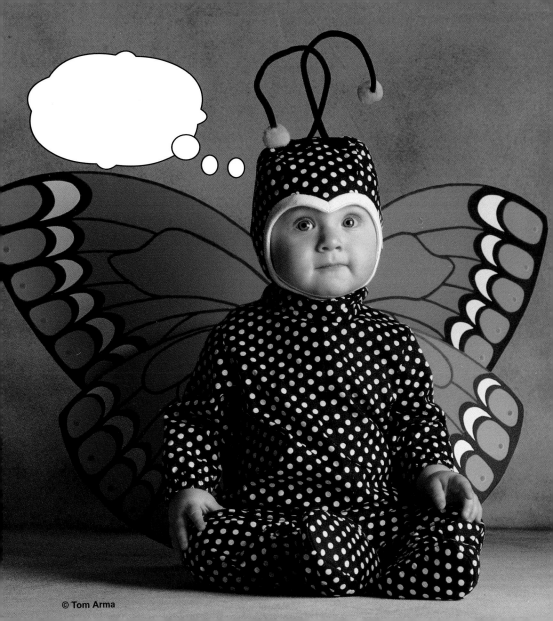

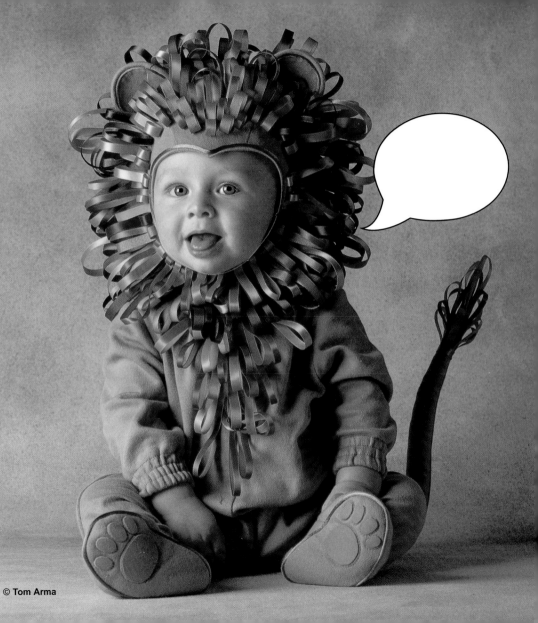

© Tom Arma

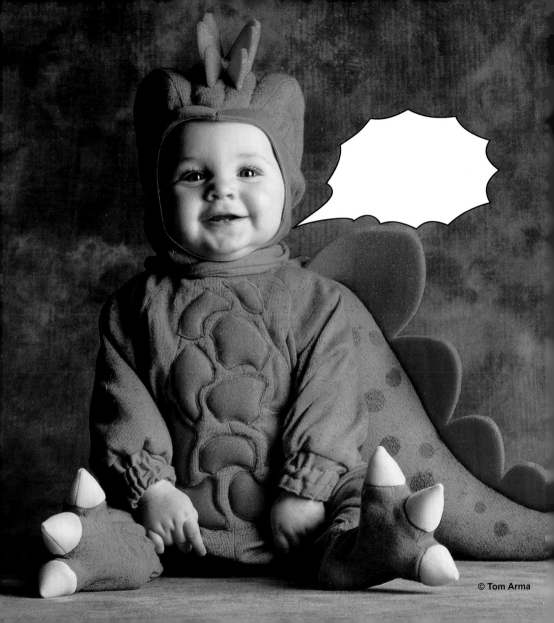

© Tom Arma

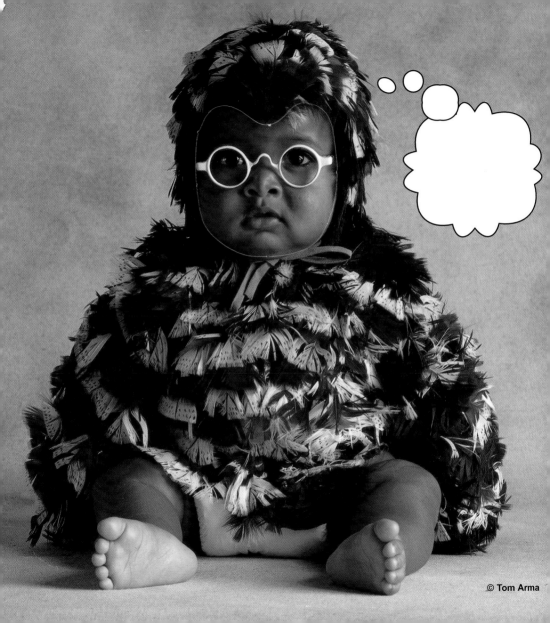

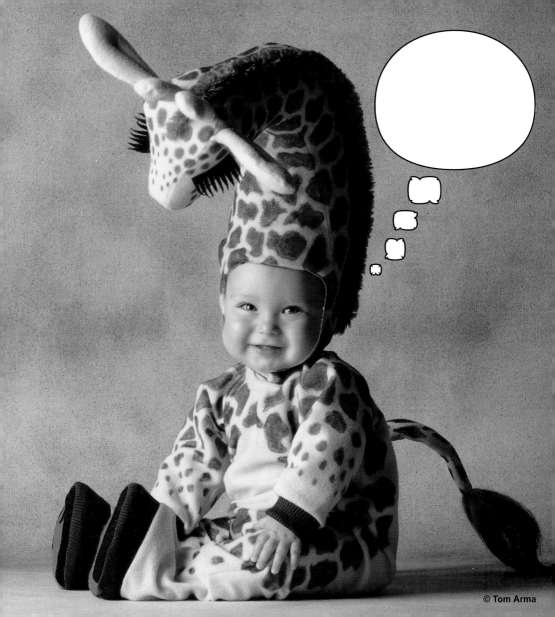

© Tom Arma

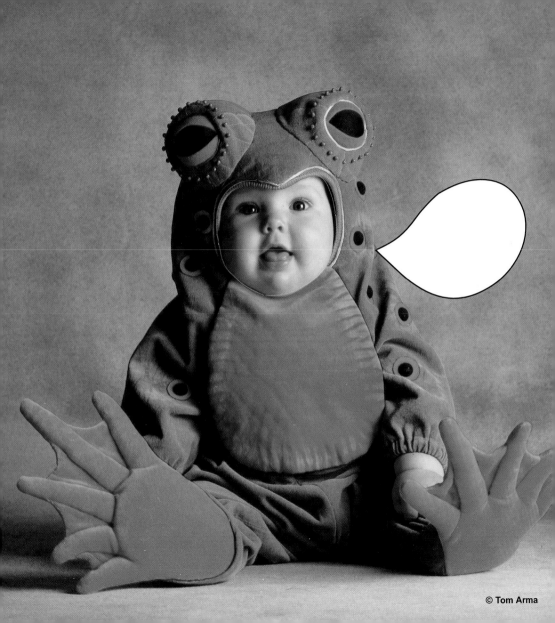

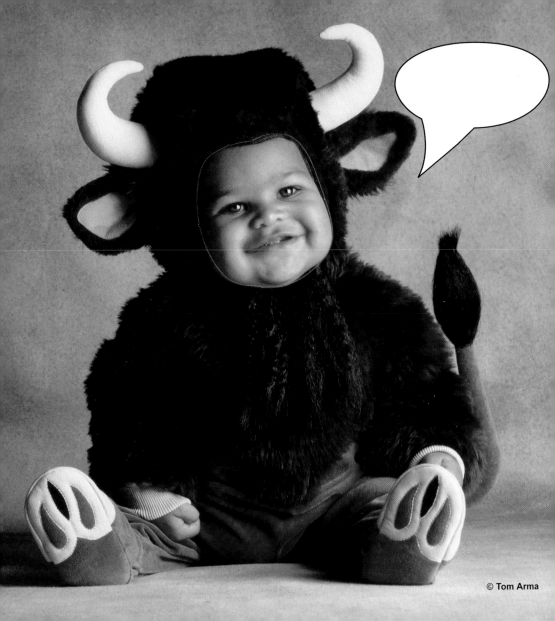

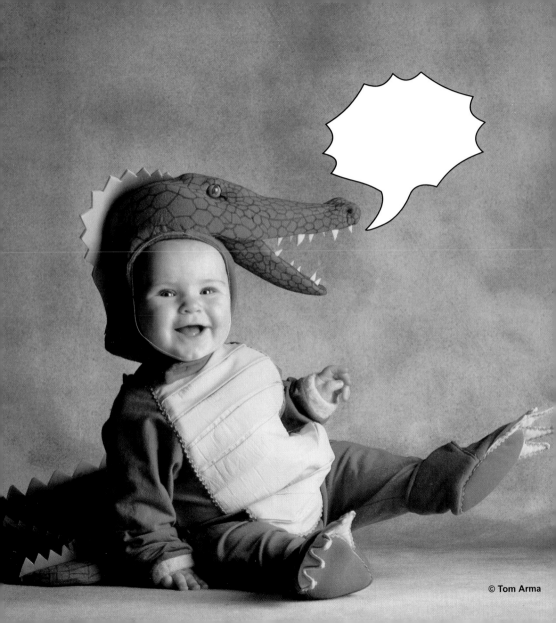

To stand up your photo frame:

- Press out a stand from the back of this page.
- Fold on the line.
- Glue or tape onto the back of the frame.

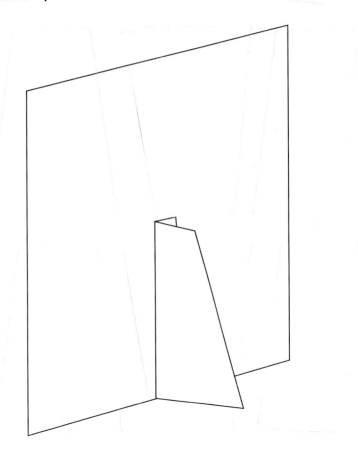

FOLD

FOLD

FOLD

FOLD

FOLD

FOLD

FOLD

FOLD

FOLD